Goodnight Selfie

First edition 2015

Library of Congress Catalog Card Number 2015932369
ISBN 978-0-7636-3182-6

15 16 17 18 19 20 APS 10 9 8 7 6 5 4 3 2 1

Printed in Humen, Dongguan, China

This book was typeset in Dina's Handwriting.
The illustrations were created digitally.

Candlewick Press
99 Dover Street
Somerville, Massachusetts 02144

visit us at www.candlewick.com

Goodnight Selfie

Scott Menchin

illustrated by Pierre Collet-Derby

CANDLEWICK PRESS

My brother just showed me how to take a selfie. (That's what you call a photo you take of yourself.) He's an expert. I got his old camera-phone when Mom and Dad got him a new one.

I tried it. One push of the button . . .

and there I am! My first selfie.

Everything I do can be a selfie.

Just-woke-up-with-crazy-hair selfie.

Brushing-my-teeth-
with-no-hands selfie.

Too-much-jam-on-
my-toast selfie.

Goldfish selfie.

Little-angel selfie.

Happy . . . mean . . . bored . . . silly . . . scary . . . crazy . . . selfies.

Skateboarding-to-school selfie.

Swinging-really-high selfie.

Boo-boo selfie.

Selfie to the right.

Selfie to the left.

Oops!

Invisible selfie.

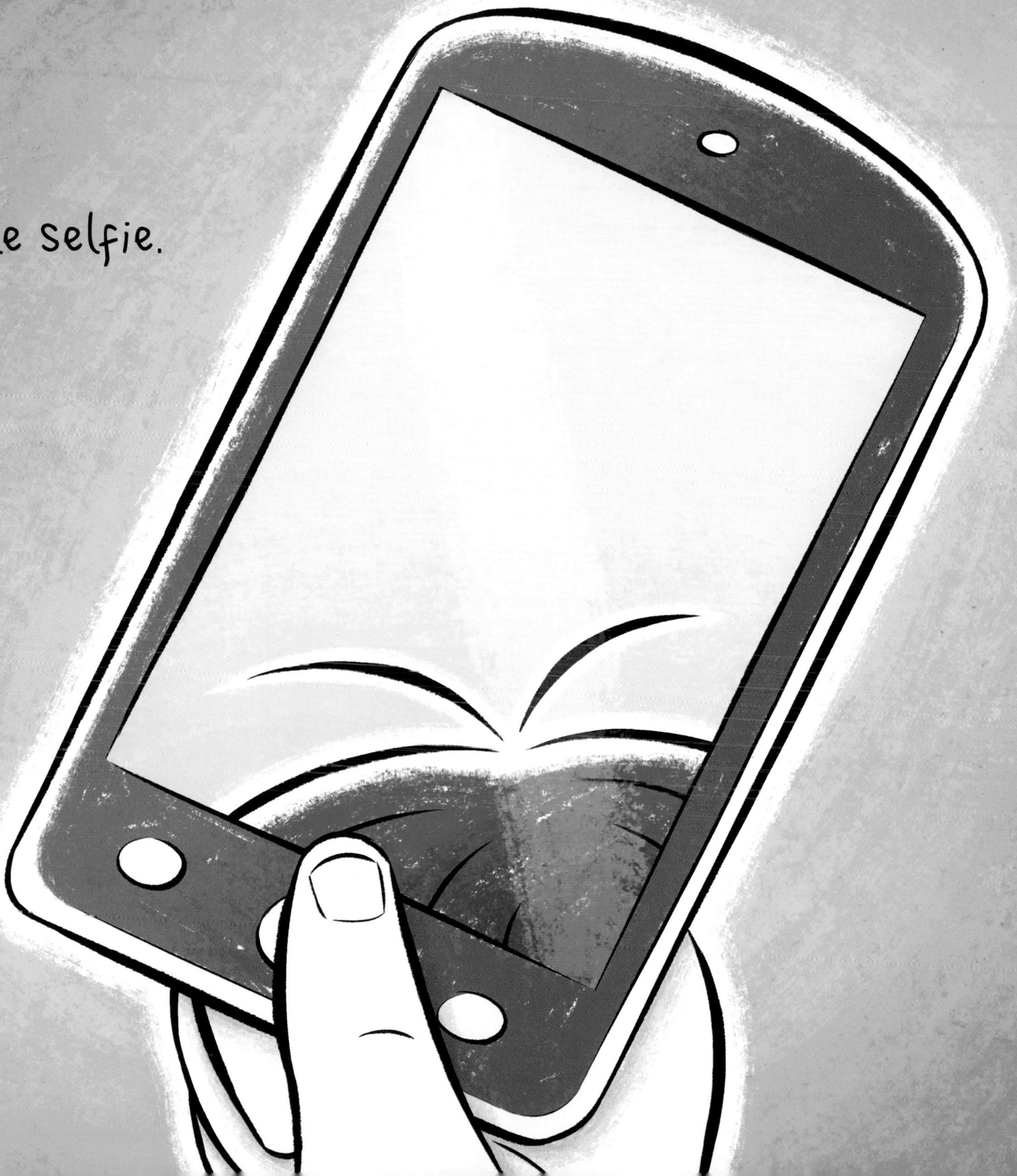

After dinner, Mom says, "Why not take a photo of someone else?" I tell her, "That would be an elsie."

Okay. Here goes.

My first elsie!

With a touch of selfie.

Elsie-selfie with Grandma Joe.

With Grandma Joe's cats.

Fancy after-my-bath selfie.

Favorite-froggy-pj's selfie.

Watching-TV-with-the-dog selfie.

"Lights-out," says Dad.

"Just one more selfie," says Mom. "You can take more tomorrow."

Only one more selfie!
What should it be?

Goodnight selfie.

To Robert Cornelius, who took the first selfie in 1839.

S. M.

To the Celebes crested macaque who took the wildest selfie in 2011.

P. C.-D.